MW00956076

IMAGINE A BROWN GIRL

Written By
Sheri Booker

Illustrated By
Baba Aminu Mustapha

For Amari Rose, may there always be joy on the other end of your dreams.
-S.J.B.

Book Her Books
An imprint of Book Her Publishing

Visit us online at
www.bookherbooks.com

Printed in the United States of America
ISBN 978-0-9727776-4-3

Somewhere on a city block
a brown girl is waiting
for the street lights to come on
so she can dream in peace.

**She can't wait to swallow
her fears for dinner,
wash away the worries of the day
and allow her imagination to come out and play.**

So when the traffic stops
and the birds are finally quiet

She closes her eyes and drifts
deep inside her imagination.

Tonight she will dream
a brown girl dream
of becoming:
a princess...
a ballerina...
a warrior...

a king...

Imagine a brown girl who can do any and everything!

She sees herself wearing a crown
as she explores the jungle fearless
and free.

Imagine a brown girl who has all the tools she can use.
She will tell the world that brown girls rule.

She reminds herself that she can be both hard and soft.

She doesn't have to choose.

She will
knock down
barriers.

She will use a bullhorn
to amplify her voice

to love...

She will break the ground
and give other little girls a
choice

to learn...

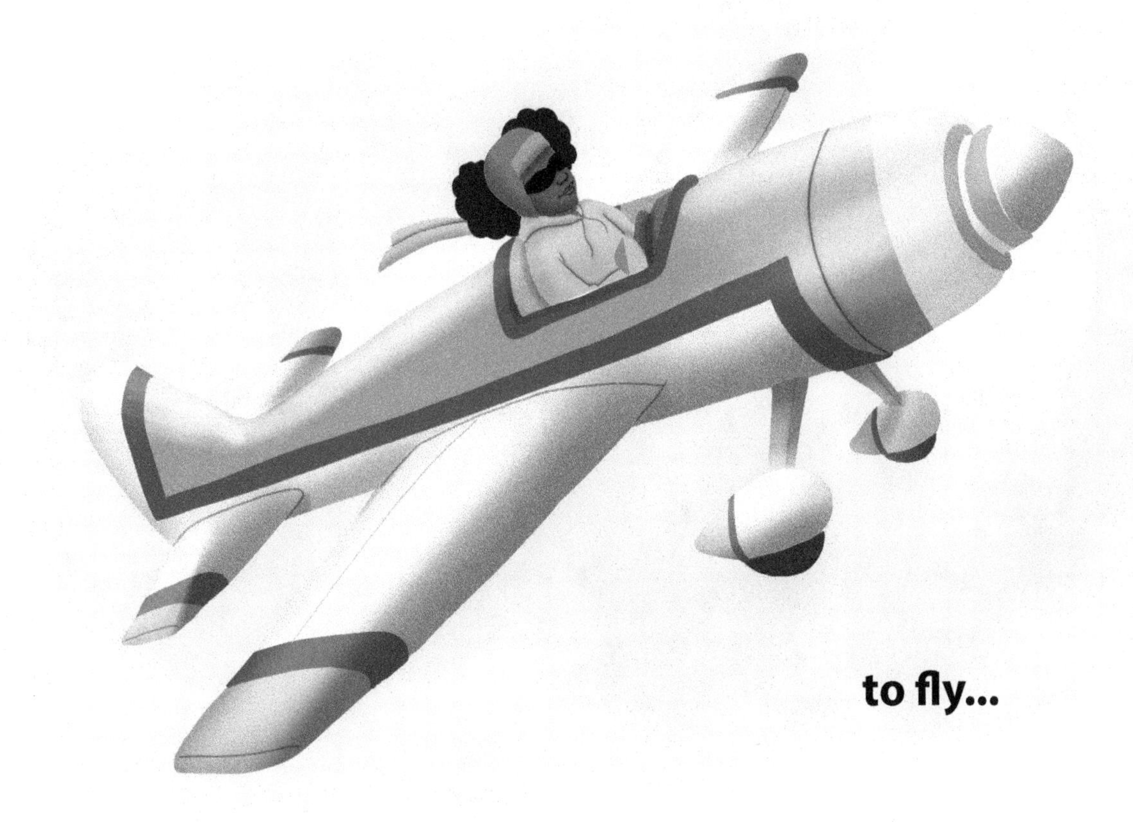

to fly...

to lead...

She will
dance with
the stars in
an African
sky.

She will jump over rainbows before landing on the moon.

She will learn to punch hard...

Become tough enough to play football.

Strong enough to move
mountains out of the way.

She will push her pride aside
and let her hair fly wild
as she always remembers her
inner child.

She will dream of being
President.

Or an international supreme court justice examining evidence.

She will spit fire like a dragon.

She will learn to turn lights on and off using only her mind.

She

will

survive.

Imagine a Brown Girl

Imagine
her
win.

Every night her dreams come alive,
she will have the power to do it again.

Tomorrow she will begin dreaming where this one ends.

Sheri Booker is a poet, writer, and educator. She is the winner of a NAACP Image Award for her memoir Nine Years Under. Her writing has appeared in Essence, Baltimore Magazine and the Baltimore Sun. She resides in Baltimore, where she teaches writing at Morgan State University.